Celebrations

Happy Father's Day!

Ada Kinney

press.

New York

Published in 2017 by The Rosen Publishing Group, Inc.
29 East 21st Street, New York, NY 10010

First Edition

Managing Editor: Nathalie Beullens-Maoui
Editor: Melissa Raé Shofner
Book Design: Michael Flynn
Illustrator: Continuum Content Solutions

Library of Congress Cataloging-in-Publication Data

Names: Kinney, Ada, author.
Title: Happy father's day! / Ada Kinney.
Description: New York : PowerKids Press, [2017] | Series: Celebrations |
   Includes index.
Identifiers: LCCN 2016025460| ISBN 9781499426687 (pbk.) | ISBN 9781499429503
   (library bound) | ISBN 9781499426694 (6 pack)
Subjects: LCSH: Father's Day–Juvenile literature.
Classification: LCC HQ756.5 .K56 2017 | DDC 394.263–dc23
LC record available at https://lccn.loc.gov/2016025460

Manufactured in the United States of America

CPSIA Compliance Information: Batch #BW17PK: For Further Information contact Rosen Publishing, New York, New York at 1-800-237-9932

Contents

Today is Father's Day!

4

I will spend the day with my dad.

We make breakfast together.
My dad makes eggs.

I make toast.

My dad likes to jog.
We often jog together.

Slow down, Dad!

Later, we go to a
baseball game.

We clap and cheer.

Our team wins the game!

I give my dad a high five.

My dad and I buy
matching hats.

Then it's time to eat pizza.

We tell jokes on the drive home.

My dad is very funny!

My dad reads me
a book before bed.
It's about kittens. He
uses silly voices.

I get sleepy when he reads.

After the story, I give
my dad a card.

I drew a picture of us.

My dad is very happy.

I love you, Dad!

Words to Know

breakfast

card

jog

Index

24